Say Goodnight to the Sleepy Animals!

Ian Whybrow   Ed Eaves

Say Goodnight to the Sleepy Animals!

MACMILLAN CHILDREN'S BOOKS

The moon is up, the stars shine bright,
Off goes Cat to say goodnight.

Out in the garden, all alone,
Who's that guarding a juicy bone?

Jack

Goodnight, Dog.
Woof, woof, woof!

Look! By the trees, it's the clever fox,
With his bushy red tail and his neat little socks.

Goodnight, Fox.
Yip, yip, yip!

High in th
Who snug

Barn Owl calls as he sails through the sky,
Say goodnight as he flies by.

Goodnight, Barn Owl.
Whit-to-whoo! Whit-to-whoo!

Who scurries by with a squeak, squeak, squeak,
Then climbs into bed with his supper in his cheek?

Goodnight, Fieldmouse.

Squeak, squeak, squeak!

Busy little rabbits, it's time to stop!
They settle in the straw with a hop, hop, flop!

Goodnight, Rabbits.

Hop, hop, flop!

Home to the kittens, softly creep,
A drink of milk and they're fast asleep.

Goodnight, Kittens.

Mew, mew, mew!

Say goodnight then, just once more
(But much quieter than before)

Goodnight, Birds!
Tweet, tweet, tweet!

Goodnight, Dog!
woof, woof, woof!

Jack

Goodnight, Fox!
Yip, yip, yip!

Goodnight, Fieldmouse!
Squeak, squeak, squeak!

Goodnight, Barn Owl!
whit-to-whoo!

Goodnight, Rabbits!
HOP, hop, flop!

Goodnight, Kittens!
Mew, mew, mew!

One last lick of her ginger fur
Goodnight, Pussycat! Purr, purr, purr.

For Amelie and Sophia with lots of love – I.W.

For Sleepy Jack and Sleepy Ralphie – E.E.

First published 2008 by Macmillan Children's Books
a division of Macmillan Publishers Limited
20 New Wharf Road, London N1 9RR
Basingstoke and Oxford
Associated companies throughout the world
www.panmacmillan.com

ISBN: 978-0-230-52799-7 (HB)
ISBN: 978-0-230-70396-4 (PB)

Text copyright © Ian Whybrow 2008
Illustrations copyright © Ed Eaves 2008
Moral rights asserted.

1 3 5 7 9 8 6 4 2

A CIP catalogue record for this book is available from the British Library.

Printed in China